j

macmillan   9/20/85   12.00

The NIGHT FLIGHT

JOANNE RYDER

Illustrated by

AMY SCHWARTZ

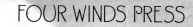

FOUR WINDS PRESS

MACMILLAN PUBLISHING COMPANY
New York

COLLIER MACMILLAN PUBLISHERS
London

Library of Congress Cataloging in Publication Data
Ryder, Joanne. The night flight.
Summary: At night after falling asleep, Anna flies to her favorite park which is now filled with crocodiles, monkeys, and a lion who takes her to his secret waterfall. 1. Children's stories, American. [1. Dreams—Fiction. 2. Night—Fiction] I. Schwartz, Amy, ill. II. Title.
PZ7.R9752Ni 1985 [E] 85-4482 ISBN 0-02-778020-1

One bright summer evening
Anna played in the park.
She sat on the back of Alexander,
the old stone lion,
and fed supper bread to the pigeons
who landed on Alexander's ears.
She dipped the long, thin crusts into the pond,
waiting while the goldfish swam closer and closer,
until she saw the park lamps glowing
and knew it was time to go home.

To Lar,
For sharing his
dreams—and the
waterfall
—J. R.

FOR
D. Z.
—A. S.

Anna ran past the rows of dark houses
till she saw her home in the grayness
and someone in a red sweater
waving at her from the stoop.
"They almost came today," Anna told Mama.
"The fish almost took the bread from my hand."

From her window Anna heard the sparrows
calling good night to each other,
calling from the three tall trees
nobody could climb.
She watched the shadows
creep up the tall buildings
and hide the trees, the street, and the city
in the dark, in the night.
Inside it was still bright;
then Papa turned out the lamp
so it was night, inside and outside.

Downstairs, the musician began to play
a smooth, sweet night song
that drifted into Anna's room.
Someone upstairs heard it too
and began to dance.
In the dark Anna listened
to the dance on her ceiling
till she closed her eyes
and dreamed of night,
of flying through the open window
into the night outside.

"Ooooooh," Anna sighed,
floating down past the windows,
down past her sleeping house
till her toes touched the cool, hard sidewalk.

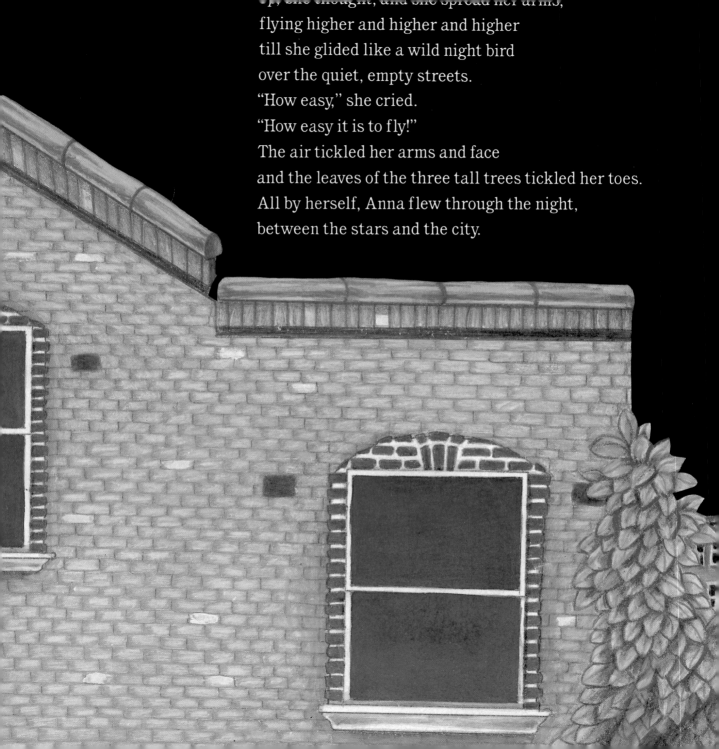

Up, she thought, and she spread her arms,
flying higher and higher and higher
till she glided like a wild night bird
over the quiet, empty streets.
"How easy," she cried.
"How easy it is to fly!"
The air tickled her arms and face
and the leaves of the three tall trees tickled her toes.
All by herself, Anna flew through the night,
between the stars and the city.

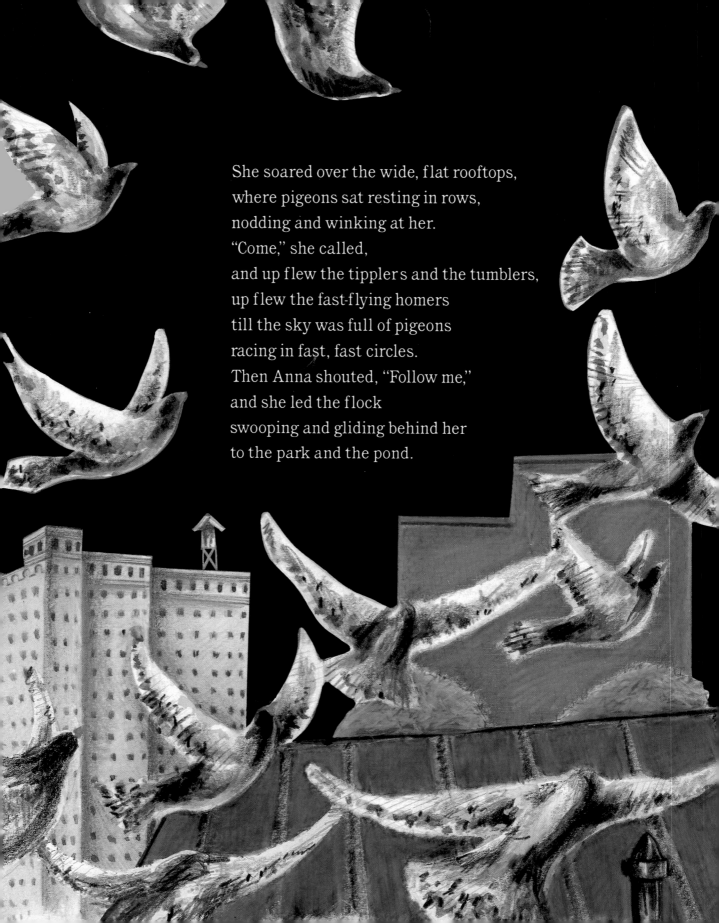

She soared over the wide, flat rooftops,
where pigeons sat resting in rows,
nodding and winking at her.
"Come," she called,
and up flew the tipplers and the tumblers,
up flew the fast-flying homers
till the sky was full of pigeons
racing in fast, fast circles.
Then Anna shouted, "Follow me,"
and she led the flock
swooping and gliding behind her
to the park and the pond.

Anna dipped low over the water,
looking down at the goldfish
who looked up at her.
"I'm thirsty," said Anna.
"Flying makes me thirsty."
So she stopped for a long, cool drink.
A black-tailed fish swam near
and said, "Swimming makes me hungry."
"Oh," sighed Anna, "and I have no bread."
The other fish came closer now,
whispering softly to her,
telling her their names,
Flicker and *Tassel* and *Billy Roundbottom*.

Suddenly the pigeons stopped drinking
and flew up into the blue-black sky.
"Goodbye," called the fish,
and they swam to the bottom of the pond.
Something's frightened them, thought Anna,
but it wasn't me.
There was no one in the park now,
no one sitting on the benches,
no one jogging around the pond.
Along the paths, the park lamps
made small circles of light.
Anna stood in one of the circles
and looked out into the blackness beyond.

She left something stir behind her
and she turned to see what had chased everyone away.
It was Alexander, real and wild,
running down the path toward her.
"Hello, Anna," said the old lion.
Anna ran to meet him
and threw her arms around his large, fluffy head.

"Climb up," said Alexander,
and they rode together
past things that rustled in the bushes.
"Crocodiles," Anna whispered.
"Lift up your feet," said the lion.
The trees grew thick
and they rode under creatures
that sighed from the branches
and snatched at Anna's hair.
"Monkeys," called Alexander. "Duck, Anna."

At the end of the trees
they rode through grass taller than they.
"Is this all in the park?" Anna asked.
"Yes," said the lion, "when you're with me."

And he took her
where the water tumbled
down and down and down.
"This is my secret place," said the lion,
and he began to roar and roar.
But all Anna could hear was
the waterfall's voice roaring louder:
Now, now, now, now,
now, now, NOW, NOW, NOW....
"Now," whispered the lion in her ear.
"It's time to go now."

They rode back faster and faster
until Anna let go and leaped into the air.
"Look, Alexander," she cried,
and the lion watched her fly
up toward the stars and the moon.

And after breakfast
Anna ran to the park,
through the people and the pigeons,
past the old stone lion sleeping quietly,
to the wide, bright pond.
And when she called their names,
the goldfish came
and nibbled the crusts right from her hand.

DAY, DAY, DAY, shouted the sun
leaping through the window,
catching Anna asleep and waking her.
"I flew," she whispered. "I really flew,"
and she sat in bed
remembering how it felt to fly,
remembering a skyful of pigeons
and a lion roaring by a waterfall.
Then in came Mama
with a good-morning hug and a good-morning kiss
and a piggyback ride all the way to breakfast.